The Princess Well-

by Pamela Oldfield

Illustrated by Glenys Ambrus

HODDER AND STOUGHTON

LONDON SYDNEY AUCKLAND TORONTO

For Dave

British Library Cataloguing in Publication Data
Oldfield, Pamela
    The Princess Well-I-May.
    I. Title   II. Ambrus, Glenys
    823'.9'1J   PZ7.04538

ISBN 0-340-23394-X (cased)
ISBN 0-340-33200-X (paperbound)

First published 1979 (cased)
First published 1983 (paperbound)

Published by Hodder and Stoughton Children's Books,
a division of Hodder and Stoughton Ltd,
Mill Road, Dunton Green, Sevenoaks, Kent TN13 2YJ

Printed in Great Britain by Springbourne Press Limited,
Basildon, Essex.

The Princess Well-I-May lived
in a tall castle.
She had beautiful red hair
and big green eyes.

Jan was a shepherd boy. He had ten woolly sheep
and he loved the Princess.
So he led his sheep up the path to the castle to ask the Princess
if she would marry him.

She looked terribly bored and gave a little yawn.
"Marry a shepherd? Well, I may –
If a dragon you should slay," she said.

So Jan found a large sword and went in search of
a small dragon.
The ten woolly sheep followed hopefully.

He soon found a handy dragon outside a cave
and made short work of it.

"You are brave," said the Princess Well-I-May,
"but are you generous?"
"I will give you anything you wish," said Jan.

The Princess smiled slyly.
"A woollen cloak is fine, I'm told
For keeping out the winter cold," she said.

The sheep were most upset!
Snip! Snap! went Jan's shears.

Then he spun the wool and began to knit it up into a cloak.
Clicketty-clack went the needles.

But when it was finished the Princess said,
"Come back tomorrow."
The next day, Jan tried again.
"Will you be my bride?" he asked her.

The Princess shrugged.
"To be your bride I'm quite inclined.
Perhaps a treasure you could find," she said.

So poor Jan borrowed a spade and began to dig.
The ten woolly sheep watched anxiously. He dug
down and down.

At the bottom of the hole he found a chest
choc-a-bloc with treasure.

He took it to the Princess Well-I-May and said,
"Now will you marry me?"
The Princess hid a smile.

"I wonder, Jan, if you could take
An apple from the giant snake?" she said.

Jan groaned. The ten woolly sheep groaned too.
Then Jan bought a giant net and went in search of
the giant snake.

And what a kerfuffle when he found it!
Swish! Woosh!

But at last the giant snake
was safely caught.

Jan picked an apple and took it back to the Princess.
She ate it in three large bites and threw the core
over her shoulder.

Jan began to wonder if he really cared for red hair
and green eyes!
But he asked her again.
"I'll marry you within a week
If you scale a mountain peak," she said.

Off marched Jan to the highest mountain.
The ten woolly sheep followed wearily.
He climbed up and up until he reached the top.
He hung his hat on the topmost peak for all to see.

The next morning he set off for the castle
wearing his second best hat.
The Princess Well-I-May giggled when she saw him.
"WILL YOU MARRY ME OR WON'T YOU?"
asked Jan crossly.
She smiled at him.

"Well, I may – within the hour –
But bring me first a golden flower," she said.
Jan lost his temper. He threw down his second
best hat and jumped on it!

Then he rushed off to look for a golden flower.

The sheep rushed after him.

He found bluebells and periwinkles in the wood.

He found primroses and violets in the hedge.
Then he found a field full of buttercups.

There was a girl in the field. She had golden curls and
blue eyes, and her arms were full of golden buttercups.

"Will you marry me, golden girl?" asked Jan.
And she said, "Yes, I will."
Just like that!